Ashlyn's Unsurprise Party

By Valerie Tripp
Illustrated by Thu Thai

★ American Girl®

Published by American Girl Publishing

21 22 23 24 25 26 27 QP 12 11 10 9 8 7 6 5 4 3

Editorial Development: Jodi Goldberg and Jennifer Hirsch
Art Direction and Design: Riley Wilkinson and Jessica Annoye
Production: Jeannette Bailey, Kristi Lively, Mary Makarushka, and Cynthia Stiles
Vignettes on pages 81–84 by Flavia Conley

americangirl.com/service

For Caroline Kerrigan Petty,
with love

Meet the WellieWishers™

The WellieWishers are a group of fun-loving girls who each have the same big, bright wish: to be a good friend. They love to play in a large and leafy backyard garden cared for by Willa's Aunt Miranda.

Willa

Ashlyn

Emerson

When the WellieWishers step into their colorful garden boots, also known as wellingtons or *wellies*, they are ready for anything—stomping in mud puddles, putting on a show, and helping friendships grow. Like you, they're learning that being kind, creative, and caring isn't always easy, but it's the best way to make friendships bloom.

Camille

Kendall

Chapter 1

Ashlyn's Surprise

Skip-skippety-skip! Ashlyn skipped into the garden. It was a bright and breezy day, and Ashlyn was in a happy hurry to join her friends, the WellieWishers. She had a *perfectly wonderful* surprise for them.

"Look, everyone," said Ashlyn. "Jump ropes! There's one for each of us."

"Hooray!" cheered Ashlyn's friends. "Thanks," they said as she handed out the ropes.

"Thank you, thank you, *thank* you,"
said Emerson, who liked to say things
three times.

Soon the WellieWishers were
jumping rope all over the garden.

Suddenly, Camille stood still. "Hey," she said. She looked at something in her hand and said again, louder, "*Hey!*"

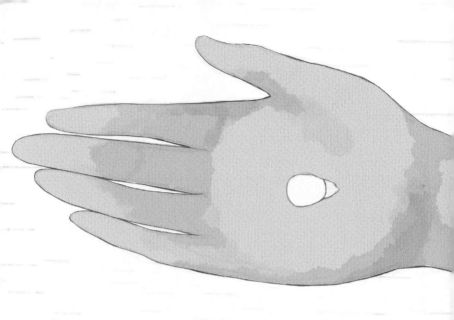

"What?" asked the girls.

"Look," said Camille. "My front tooth fell out."

"Let's see!" squealed her friends. They gathered around Camille to look at the fallen-out tooth. "Oooooh," they cooed.

"How'd it happen?" asked Kendall.

"Well," said Camille, "I just wiggled it. Like this." Camille opened her mouth and wiggled her other front tooth to show the girls. Then she made up a little rhyme:

> I wiggled it
> And jiggled it
> A little bit.
> Just wiggled it
> And jiggled it
> A little bit.

And her friends asked:

> You wiggled it
> And jiggled it
> A little bit?
> Just wiggled it
> And jiggled it
> A little bit?

And Camille wiggled her other front tooth some more, and answered:

> Yup, wiggled it
> And jiggled it
> A little—*hey*!

Camille stopped singing. "Yiketh!" she said with a brand-new lisp. "Look—my *other* front tooth came out!"

Chapter 2

Two-Too

Oh, you lucky duck," said Emerson. "Two teeth in one day!"

"Now the tooth fairy will find *two* teeth under your pillow," said Ashlyn.

Camille smiled, and all the WellieWishers grinned at her.

"Now your smile is bigger than ever!" said Kendall.

"Yeth," said Camille. She sighed.
"Maybe I thouldn't have wiggled and

jiggled tho much. I'll mith thothe
teeth. I've had them thince I wath
a baby."

Ashlyn could tell that Camille wasn't entirely happy about losing her teeth. She wished she could make Camille feel better.

Suddenly, Ashlyn had an idea. The WellieWishers should have a party! A party always made everyone feel better about everything.

"Let's celebrate," Ashlyn said, clasping her hands together. "Let's have a party. We'll call it the Two-Teeth-Out Tea Party. Would you like that, Camille?"

"Oh, *yeth*," said Camille. "I love partieth."

"And after the tea party we'll have a sleepover, if Aunt Miranda says it's okay," said Ashlyn. "We'll sleep out under the stars."

"A sleepover! Hooray!" cheered the WellieWishers.

Ashlyn smiled. She could picture every single teeny, tiny detail of her party for Camille. Everything would be *just so.*

As she imagined her party, Ashlyn made up a little rhyme:

Oh, the sun will shine
in a bright blue sky, just so.
My friends will be happy
and so will I, just so.

We'll wear best dresses and
flowery crowns, just so.
We'll eat pretty treats that
we pass around, just so.

Oh, everything will be
just so won-der-ful-ly,
just so perfectly
just so!

Ashlyn couldn't wait. The
WellieWishers would be so pleased—
and so surprised.

"A tea and sleepover party! Oh, I *love* it, it's *won*derful!" exclaimed Emerson, twirling. "Let's put on a show all about teeth. We can recite Camille's 'wiggle, jiggle' rhyme, and we can pretend to be tooth fairies. We'll call our show 'Two Too-Loose Tooths.' Get it? We'll wear tutus, and—"

"Well," Ashlyn began, "your idea is funny, but it's not—"

Kendall interrupted. "I'll decorate the wagon, and Camille can ride in it."

"*No*," said Ashlyn, "I already—"

Willa piped up. "We could have the
party in the woods," she said. "We can
use a tree stump as a table, and eat
berries and honey, and—"

"NO!" said Ashlyn. And this time, she stamped her foot.

The other WellieWishers were quiet.
They looked at Ashlyn.

Ashlyn's face was pink. She took
a deep breath and said, "It's nice of
you to offer to help. But the party
was my idea, and I want it to be *just
so.*" Ashlyn recited her rhyme to her
friends:

> Oh, the sun will shine
> in a bright blue sky, just so.
> You will all be happy
> and so will I, just so.
>
> We'll wear best dresses
> and flowery crowns, just so.
> We'll eat pretty treats that
> we pass around, just so.

Oh, everything will be
just so won-der-ful-ly,
just so perfectly
just so!

"Yes, but—" Emerson began.

"I already have it all planned,"
Ashlyn interrupted. "I'll do it all
myself." She explained, "I want to

keep my plans secret, because I want the party to be full of surprises for all of you."

"Well," said Willa. "Okay, I guess."

"Don't futh too much," said Camille.

"I can't *believe* that you don't want a show," said Emerson, shaking her head.

"Ask for help if you need it," said Kendall.

But Ashlyn was already hurrying away to ask Aunt Miranda if they could have a sleepover. She couldn't *wait* to begin getting ready for her party.

Chapter 3

The Secret Plan

The next day, the WellieWishers received invitations from Ashlyn.

Come to the
Two Teeth Out
Tea Party

Slumber Party
for Camille on Saturday!
Bring your pajamas and your sleeping bag!

"Aren't they nithe?" said Camille.

"Yes, I *love* them. They're *won*derful!" said Emerson.

"I'm glad Aunt Miranda gave permission for a sleepover," said Willa. "I love to sleep out under the stars in my sleeping bag. Don't you?"

"Oh, yes," said Kendall.

"I prefer sleeping in a tent," said Emerson. "How about you, Camille?"

But before Camille could answer, the girls heard a teeny, tiny "ouch."

The girls crept to the corner of the playhouse. They peeked around and saw Ashlyn with a big bunch of roses.

Emerson whispered, "Poor Ashlyn! She must

have hurt her finger on a thorn."

"Oh, dear, that'th too bad," Camille sighed softly.

"Someone should help her," said Willa.

"Ashlyn said she didn't want any help," said Kendall. "She wants to keep her plan a secret."

"Maybe *we* could have a secret plan, too," said Emerson. "And our secret plan would be—"

"—to help Ashlyn!" said all the girls at once.

They grinned at one another.

The girls put their secret plan into action right away.

Emerson whistled as she waltzed around the corner of the playhouse. "Oh!" she said, as if she were surprised to see Ashlyn. "Hi, Ashlyn! How's it going?"

"Fine," said Ashlyn. "I'm making flower crowns for everyone."

"Oh, how pretty," said Emerson, looking at the flowers. "But don't forget that roses make Willa sneeze."

"They do?" said Ashlyn. "Oh, *no*." Her party wouldn't be perfect if Willa was sneezing all the time!

"Hey, I have an idea," said Emerson. "I could make Willa a crown out of paper stars instead."

"But—" said Ashlyn.

"Please?" said Emerson. "I love stars!"

"Well, okay," said Ashlyn. She grinned. "We don't want Willa ah-chooooing, doooo we?"

"Nooo!" Emerson smiled. "It wouldn't be pleeeeasing if she were sneeeezing."

As Emerson put stars on the crown, she made up a little poem:

Don't put a rose by Willa's nose
Or Willa will be sneezing.
Ah-choo, ah-choo will never do.
Sneezing isn't pleasing!

Ashlyn laughed. "Thanks, Emerson," she said. She was a teeny, tiny bit sorry that a teeny, tiny bit of her surprise party would be *un*surprising for Emerson. But she was glad that it would be better for Willa.

A little while after Emerson left, Willa trip-trotted around the corner of the playhouse. "Oh!" she said, as if she were surprised to see Ashlyn. "Hi, Ashlyn! How's it going?"

"Fine," said Ashlyn. "I'm putting nuts in cups for everyone."

"I love nuts!" said Willa. "But nuts make Kendall break out in itchy,

scratchy, bright red spots."

"They do?" said Ashlyn. "Oh, *no.*" Her party wouldn't be perfect if Kendall broke out in red spots!

"Hey, I have an idea," said Willa. "I could put a little sign on Kendall's nut cup that says: 'For the Squirrels.'"

"But—" said Ashlyn.

"Please?" said Willa. "You know how I love to feed the squirrels."

"Well, okay," said Ashlyn. She grinned. "We don't want Kendall to be spotty and dotty."

"Absolutely notty," agreed Willa.
As she printed the sign, Willa made up
a little poem:

> The squirrels must eat
> Kendall's nuts
> Or Kendall will get spotty.
> Does Kendall want an itchy rash?
> Ab-so-lute-ly notty!

Ashlyn laughed. "Thanks, Willa," she said. She was a teeny, tiny bit sorry that a teeny, tiny bit of her surprise party would be *un*surprising for Willa. But she was glad that it would be better for Kendall.

A little while after Willa left, Kendall strolled slowly around the corner of the playhouse. "Oh!" she said, as if she were surprised to see Ashlyn. "Hi, Ashlyn! How's it going?"

"Fine," said Ashlyn. "I'm clearing space for our sleeping bags."

"I can't wait to sleep under the stars!" said Kendall. "But Emerson prefers to sleep in a tent."

"She does?" said Ashlyn. "Oh, *no*."
Her party wouldn't be perfect if Emerson
wasn't content without a tent!

"Hey, I have an idea!" said Kendall.
"I could *make* a tent for Emerson."

"But—" said Ashlyn.

"Please?" said Kendall. "You know
how I love to make stuff."

"Well, okay," said Ashlyn. She smiled.
"We want Emerson to be happy."

"So I'll make a tent and make it
snappy," said Kendall with a grin.
As Kendall put the tent together,
she made up a little poem:

Emerson must have a tent
Or else she won't be happy.
I'll pitch a tent and make it snug
and also make it snappy!

Ashlyn laughed. "Thanks, Kendall," she said. She was a teeny, tiny bit sorry that a teeny, tiny bit of her surprise party would be *un*surprising for Kendall. But she was glad that it would be better for Emerson.

A little while after Kendall left, Camille skipped casually around the corner of the playhouse. "Oh!" she said, as if she were surprised to see Ashlyn. "Hi, Athlyn! How'th it going?"

"Fine," said Ashlyn. "I'm shining apples for everyone."

"That'th nithe!" said Camille.

"Oh, *no*," said Ashlyn when she heard Camille's lisp. "I forgot that you don't have any front teeth, so you can't eat an apple." Her party wouldn't be perfect if the guest of honor, Camille, couldn't eat the food!

"Hey, I have an idea," said Camille.

"On the day of the party, I could athk Aunt Miranda to cut the apple for me, and then I could eat it."

"That's a good idea," said Ashlyn. She grinned. "Aunt Miranda will cut up the apple so that you can eat it slice by slice."

"That'll be nithe!" laughed Camille. Ashlyn said a little poem to her:

> You have lost your
> two front teeth.
> Your food must come in slices.
> If your apple's cut apart,
> That will be the nicest.

"Thankth, Athlyn," Camille said as she left.

Ashlyn was a teeny, tiny bit sorry that a teeny, tiny bit of her surprise party would be *un*surprising for Camille, but she was glad that it would be better for her.

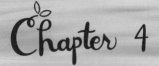

Chapter 4

Time for the Party

On Saturday, the WellieWishers came to the garden in their very best party dresses.

"Ooooooh," they sighed with admiration when they saw Ashlyn's decorations.

"The tea table looks beautiful, Ashlyn," said Willa.

"Yes, I *love* it! It's *wonderful!*" exclaimed Emerson.

"I like how you've folded our napkins specially for us," said Kendall. "They're in the shapes of things that we love."

"Aunt Miranda showed me how," said Ashlyn, giving each girl a crown.

"Thanks for remembering that roses make me sneeze," said Willa.

"I didn't remember," said Ashlyn. "Emerson did. Emerson said,

> Don't put a rose by Willa's nose
> Or Willa will be sneezing.
> *Ah-choo, ah-choo* will never do.
> Sneezing isn't pleasing!"

"You remembered that nuts make me break out in red spots," said Kendall.

"Nope," said Ashlyn, "that was Willa. She said:

> The squirrels must eat
> Kendall's nuts
> Or Kendall will get spotty.
> Does Kendall want an itchy rash?
> Ab-so-lute-ly notty!"

"Did you remember that I like to sleep in a tent?" asked Emerson.

"Kendall did," said Ashlyn. "She said,

> Emerson must have a tent
> Or else she won't be happy.
> I'll pitch a tent and make it snug
> and also make it snappy!"

"Well, it was *you* who remembered that I have no front teeth," said Camille, who by now had figured out how to talk without a lisp. "You said:

You have lost your
two front teeth.
Your food must come in slices.
If your apple's cut apart,
That will be the nicest.

And it was *you* who worked very hard
to make the party wonderful! Thank
you, Ashlyn."

"Yes, thank you, Ashlyn!" said all
the other WellieWishers.

"Thank *you*!" said Ashlyn. She
smiled at the girls. "You all helped
me." She laughed, saying, "And you
know what? It was way more fun
when you were helping me, even

though it means that the party is kind of unsurprising for you."

"It's an *un*surprise party!" cheered the WellieWishers. "We love it!" And all the girls chanted along with Ashlyn:

The sun is shining in a
bright blue sky, just so.
My friends are all happy
and so am I, just so.

We're wearing best dresses
and flowery crowns, just so.
We'll eat pretty treats that
we pass around, just so.

Oh, everything we see
is just so won-der-ful-ly,
just so perfectly
just so!

63

Chapter 5

Surprise at the *Unsurprise* Party

The girls were having a terrific time until . . .

Plip, Plip, Plip,

Swoosh! A gusty wind whooshed through the garden, blowing the napkins and flowers off the tea table and toppling the tower of treats.

Gush! Buckets of rain poured down, drenching the girls in their dresses and making the tent collapse in the middle and fall to the ground like a soggy puddle.

Crrr-ack! Lightning ripped the sky in two.

Ka-Boom! Thunder shook the ground and rattled the teacups in their saucers.

As quickly as they could, the girls dashed into the playhouse.

"I'm soaked!" exclaimed Emerson.

"Me, too," said Willa.

"I'm as wet as a fish!" said Camille.

"I'm as squishy as a sponge!" said
Kendall.

Ashlyn didn't say anything. She
started to cry.

Camille patted Ashlyn on the back. "Say what's making you sad," she said gently.

Ashlyn gulped. "The party is ruined," she sobbed. "I hate this rain. It ruined *everything*."

"Not *everything*, Ashlyn," said Willa in her soft voice. "It didn't ruin the trees and flowers. They *need* the rain."

"And just think," said Camille, "when the rain stops, there may be a rainbow, and puddles to play in."

"Meanwhile, we're safe and cozy inside," said Kendall.

"We're not cozy," said Ashlyn, sniffling a big sniffle. "We're soaking wet, and shivering, and—"

"Oh, oh, oh!" said Emerson. "I have just had the *best* idea. Let's ask Aunt Miranda if we can have the party in her house in front of the fireplace!

It will be the Two-Teeth-Out-in-PJs Tea Party and Sleepover!"

"Yes!" cheered the other girls. Emerson's new name for the party had such a funny tongue-twistery sound that they all had to laugh—even Ashlyn.

Chapter 6

Just So

The girls scurried through the rain to Aunt Miranda's house. While Aunt Miranda made a cozy fire, they changed into their pajamas and dried their hair. Then they sat by the fire in their pajamas and munched their apples.

Camille sighed happily. "Leave it to Ashlyn to throw the most fun party ever," she said.

"No," said Ashlyn. "Leave it to the WellieWishers. We did this *together*."

Suddenly, Ashlyn started to laugh.

"What's funny?" asked Emerson.

"This party," said Ashlyn. She asked questions, and the WellieWishers answered:

"Is the sun shining bright in a bright blue sky?"

"Well, no."

"But are you unhappy, or am I?"

"Well, no."

"Are we in best dresses and flowery crowns?"

"Well, no."

"Do we have pretty treats to pass around?"

"Well, no."

"But even so, things are just so won-der-ful-ly, just so perfectly *just so!*"

Ashlyn smiled at her friends. "This party did not turn out at *all* the way I thought it would."

"So in a way," she added, "it *was* a surprise party after all!"

Let's Have a Party!

A party makes any occasion special, and having a party is a memorable way to celebrate a child's developmental milestone. It's also a perfect way to turn an occasion that may prompt ambivalent feelings—like losing two teeth at one time!—into a happy one.

Party planning

How many to invite? An easy rule of thumb is to have the same number of guests as your girl's age. If there's another adult on hand to help out, the guest list can be a bit longer.

How long should it last? For three- and four-year-olds, 60 to 90 minutes is enough. For five- and six-year-olds, 90 minutes to two hours. If your child is old enough to help with setup and cleanup, consider the time you'll need for those tasks as well.

What about slumber parties? Sleepovers are usually best for girls age eight and up, unless they know one another really well or have slept over before. For younger girls, keep it to just a few guests, and be prepared in case someone wants to go home early.

Invite her to help

Ashlyn wanted to do everything herself—but she discovered that sharing the work made the party much better. Like the WellieWishers, your daughter will want to join the fun of party preparations, so let her help. She can choose the decor theme or colors, and help set the table and decorate the room with flowers, stuffed animals, or paper decorations.

Festive food

If the party has a theme, you don't have to go all out with elaborate decorations. Your girl and her guests will be just as delighted by a few easy, fun foods that carry the theme. For example:

❀ **Sandwich shapes:** Make thin sandwiches, such as butter and jam, bologna, or cheese on soft bread. Use cookie cutters to trim the sandwiches into shapes that fit the party theme, such as leaves and flowers for a fairy theme, or fish and starfish for a mermaid theme.

❀ **Very berry punch:** Mix 2 parts apple-raspberry juice with 1 part sparkling water. Float fresh raspberries on the top. Add some frozen-juice ice cubes or a few scoops of raspberry sherbet to keep it chilled.

Other kid pleasers are make-your-own ice cream sundaes (set out a few flavors of ice cream and toppings) or decorate-your-own cupcakes (set out cupcakes, frosting, and a variety of sprinkles). These can get messy, so keep a sponge handy, or set up the dessert station at an outdoor table.

Group activities

For younger children, cooperative games and activities work better than competitive ones. A few ideas:

* **Make a mural:** Tape a long piece of butcher paper to a table, floor, or wall. Set out crayons and colored pencils; suggest a theme such as zoo, ocean, magic forest, or whatever ties with the party theme; and watch the kids create a masterpiece!

✿ **Seek and go hide:** While everyone else waits in the kitchen, one person hides somewhere in the house. Then they all spread out to search. Anyone who finds the hiding person silently hides with her. By the end, the last person will find all the kids squished into the hiding spot, giggling like crazy!

✿ **Stuffed animal parade:** Have the guests dress up stuffed animals using ribbons, yarn, feathers, and fabric scraps. (You may need to help out with scissors and tape.) Then play marching music and have a parade to show off the fancy animals!

✿ **Mirror, mirror:** Sit in a circle and have one girl make a goofy face at the girl next to her. That girl then makes the same face to the girl next to her, and so on. See how much the face has changed by the time it's back to the first girl!

About the Author

VALERIE TRIPP says that she became
a writer because of the kind of person she is.
She says she's curious, and writing requires you
to be interested in everything. Talking is her
favorite sport, and writing is a way of talking
on paper. She's a daydreamer, which helps her
come up with her ideas. And she loves words.
She even loves the struggle to come up
with just the right words as she writes
and rewrites. Ms. Tripp lives in
Maryland with her husband.